TWO BICYCLES IN BEIJING

BE A FRIEND !

T. ROBESON

何顥思

Teresa Robeson   illustrated by *Junyi Wu*

Albert Whitman & Company
Chicago, Illinois

One, two; yi, er.

Side by side, Lunzi and Huangche
came out of the factory.

One, two; yi, er.

Side by side, Lunzi and Huangche sat
in a bicycle shop in Beijing.

They leaned to the left together and
gazed at the world together.

They watched people bustle past and traffic whiz by.

They watched customers enter the shop, pick out bicycles, and leave.

They wished they could stay like this forever.

But one day…

a girl with a sky-blue sweater and cloud-white apron came into the shop.

She sat on some of the bikes.

She ran her fingers along their frames.

Her eyes lit up when she saw Huangche. "That is the perfect bike," she said. "The sun to my sky."

She paid for Huangche and wheeled him out the door.

Oh no! thought Lunzi.
She tipped over.

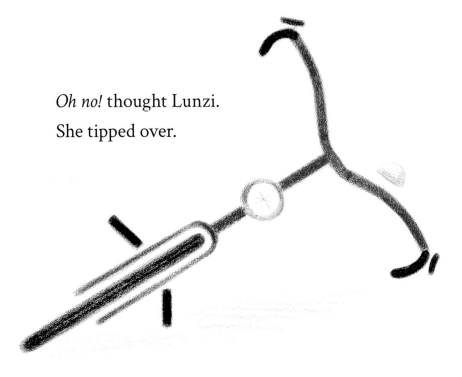

As the store clerk propped Lunzi back up, a boy entered the shop. He wore a messenger bag and a cheerful smile that grew even bigger when he saw Lunzi.

"That is the perfect bike," he said. "A zesty red as I zip around the city to make deliveries."

Lunzi's hopes rose. *Hurry, hurry,* she thought. *I can still find Huangche if we hurry.*

The boy wheeled Lunzi outside and hopped on.

Brrr-ring-ring!

Watch out! Lunzi wove through the crowds in the narrow hutong.

Brrr-ring-ring-ring! Lunzi turned onto the main road from the alley. The wider jie was also bustling with people.

Where could Huangche have gone?

Ducks took to the sky in a
panic as Lunzi raced by
Nanguan Park. She zoomed
onto a dajie, mirroring the
flight of the ducks.

Lunzi spied a flash of
yellow to the right.

Could that be Huangche?

No.

It was only the yellow
purse of someone entering
the National Art Museum.

They veered left, dipping south
with the curve of the road…

another flash of yellow! Could that be Huangche?

It was the yellow clothes of
performers darting and spinning
in a martial arts dance outside
the gates of the Forbidden City.

Lunzi cycled on, through Beihai Park as the ducks landed in a pond.

Yellow, yellow! Could that be Huangche?

No. It was only the golden
tail of a child's kite, twirling
in the autumn air.

Past the park, traffic hummed
and traffic roared.

Yellow here and yellow there…
but they were cars and jackets and store signs.
Millions of bicycles in Beijing and none was Lunzi's friend.

Brrr-ring-ring. They were at the Beijing Concert Hall now.

A glint of yellow! Was that Huangche?

Still no.

It was only yellow chrysanthemums
outside the building—soft, buttery dots
in the late afternoon light.

Past Tiananmen Square they flew…no yellow at all.

"Time to go home now, my
pretty red bicycle," said the boy.
"All my deliveries are done."

They turned westward. Lunzi rolled—a little slow,
a little wobbly. The day had been an adventure,
but her heart ached for Huangche.

The boy stopped
at a shop to buy
pastries for dinner.
Lunzi leaned
against the brick
wall with a sigh.

Then—a whoosh of yellow, just ahead.
It was probably nothing.

Brrring-ring-ring!

Could it be?

It was!

The girl with the sky-blue
sweater wheeled her sunny
yellow bicycle out from
the alley, and leaned it

face-to-face

with Lunzi.

Lunzi and Huangche grinned
from handlebar to handlebar.

"Ni hao!" said the boy.
"Your bike was in the
 shop next to mine!"

"I remember it,"
 said the girl.

"Would you like a bao?"
 the boy offered.

The girl laughed a
tinkling laugh, like the
sound of a bicycle bell.

Yi, er...yi, er;

one, two…one, two.

Side by side,

old friends   and new.

GLOSSARY
of Mandarin Chinese Terms

bao 包: bun; pastry

dajie 大街: big street; avenue

huangche 黃車: yellow bicycle or vehicle

hutong 胡同: the literal translation is "alley,"
but they are more like very small roads,
filled with traffic and sometimes storefronts

jie 街: street

lunzi 輪子: wheel

ni hao 你好: the literal translation is "you good,"
but this is used to mean "How are you?"

Beijing *and* Its Sights

Beijing 北京

北 means "north" and 京 means "capital."

Historians think that Beijing was originally established as a trading town more than four thousand years ago. Emperors have used it as the center of government for about two thousand of those years, building magnificent palaces and beautiful temples there. Beijing, as the capital of China, is still the center of government today.

Nanguan Park 南馆公園

"South Hall Park" or "South Pavilion Hall"

A small park in the northeast corner of Beijing, Nanguan Park is special because it was the first ecological garden to use reclaimed water when it was created in 1956. A treatment station within the park processes wastewater from nearby neighborhoods. The cleaned water feeds the park pond, and waters the trees and flowers.

Beihai Park 北海公園

"North Ocean Park"

First built more than one thousand years ago, the park got its name from the large, ocean-like pond within. For centuries, only emperors and their families were allowed to use this imperial garden. But in 1925, after the last dynastic rule, the garden was opened to the public.

Tiananmen Square 天安門廣場

"Gate of Heavenly Peace Square"

Named for the Gate of Heavenly Peace to its north, this important public area in the center of Beijing houses the mausoleum of Chairman Mao, China's longtime leader.

For my husband, kids, sister, and father, who toured
our ancestral homeland with me, though not on bicycles
—TR

For Chris, who's been there for me on every road I've taken
—JW

Library of Congress Cataloging-in-Publication data is on file with the publisher.

Text copyright © 2020 by Teresa Robeson
Illustrations copyright © 2020 by Albert Whitman & Company
Illustrations by Junyi Wu
First published in the United States of America in 2020 by Albert Whitman & Company
ISBN 978-0-8075-0764-3 (hardcover)
ISBN 978-0-8075-0765-0 (ebook)

Printed in China
10 9 8 7 6 5 4 3 2 1 WKT 24 23 22 21 20 19
Design by Aphelandra Messer

For more information about Albert Whitman & Company,
visit our website at www.albertwhitman.com.